Clint Faraday
book thirty six
Deadly Game

Clint is talking with friends in David. A man from Oklahoma says he's thinking about getting in a game of poker with some people he met from Panamá City and Tampa, Florida.

Clint had heard of Rodriguez when he was in Florida. He had a run-in or two with him.

He warned the man to stay away from those people. They were violent hoods.

Some people just *won't* listen!

Contents

A Trip to Town   pg.   1
All Bets Off!   pg.   7
What Stakes?   pg.   15
Place Your Bet!   pg.   23
New Deck!   pg.   34
Bluff or Fold?   pg.   39
Redeal   pg.   46
Dealer Folds!   pg.   61

About the author

CD Moulton has traveled extensively over much of the world both in the music business, where he was a rock guitarist, songwriter and arranger and in an import/export business. He has been everything from a bar owner to auto salvage (junkyard) manager, longshoreman to high steel worker, orchid grower to landscaper, tropical fish farmer to commercial fisherman. He started writing books in 1983 and has published more than 350 books as of January 1, 2023. His most popular books to date are about research with orchids, though much of his science fiction and fantasy work has proven popular. He wrote the CD Grimes, PI series, and the Det. Nick Storie series, Clint Faraday series, and many other works.

He now resides in Gualaca, Chiriqui, Panamá, where he writes books, plays music with friends, does research with orchids and medicinal plants. He has lately become involved in fighting for the rights of the indigenous people, who are among his closest friends, and in fighting the extreme corruption in the courts and police in Panamá.

He offers the free e-book, *Fading Paradise*, that explains what he has been through because of the corruption.

CD is the discoverer of the Chadam Protocol for curing cancer.

Facebook page Ambrosia peruviana for cancer.

A Trip to Town

Clint Faraday, retired PI from Florida, now living in Panamá, got off the bus from Soloy to David and stretched. It seemed a bit hot here in David, but he had been in the mountains in the comarca at his place near Quebrada Tula for the past three months and had acclimated to the coolness of the forest at that altitude.

He was the only gringo-looking person on the bus. He had been declared Ngobe by the council and was now an Indio, and proud to be. He came to David once a month to buy supplies and check on what was going on in the world. He would stay tonight and possibly tomorrow night, then return to the comarca.

He tossed his backpack across his shoulder and walked leisurely to Pensión Costa Rica, where he often stayed when in David. He chatted awhile with Lee, the owner, went to his room to clean up and took a taxi to Las Brasas for a superb rib-eye dinner. He talked with a couple of people there he knew from earlier trips. There was a gringo, a man from Oklahoma, who was with two of the native Panamanians he knew. He was invited to join them for an afterdinner beer.

After about twenty minutes, the Oklahoma man, Danny Betts, said he had to go. He was in an all-night poker session with some Panamanians and two men from Florida. Tampa.

"I spent a bit of time in Tampa. It's just another big, loud, dirty city to me. I prefer the comarca. David's the only city I've ever liked," Clint said. "It's not like a city."

"True," Danny replied. "I kind of like it, but I prefer places like Vegas or Tahoe. Places where the days are for sleeping and the nights are for partying.

"You were a detective in Florida? Maybe you ran across my poker playing opponents. Mike Rodriguez and Henry Calhoun?"

"Rodriguez owns that bar near the causeway?"

"I think he said he owns a couple of bars."

"I'd advise against getting involved with them. They're reputed to be Cosa Nostra bigshots. I know Rodriguez is bad news. Calhoun, I only know of by reputation. If they're here, it's not for any reason I'd find acceptable.

"Don't get tied up with those two in any way. They'll use you for a goat if anything goes wrong. I know how they operate."

"It's just for a game of poker. I'm not involved with them in anything else."

"That you know of. I'm serious."

"We'll see what happens. Got to go!" He shook hands around and left. Clint sighed and shook his head sadly. "That one's in 'way over his head and doesn't have sense enough to know it!"

"He's of age," Glena said. "He wanted me to go with him for luck, but I don't care to sit around being bored all night so he can have good luck."

They chatted a bit, then Clint went to the Costa Rica to get a good night's sleep. In the morning he went to the area around the bus terminal to buy the things he needed. They're better quality and cheaper there. It's where everyone from the fincas gets agricultural supplies of all types. The vegetable wholesalers are there, so you can walk in off the streets and save a lot by shopping there. Many of the Indios only go into that area for specific things, then return by bus to wherever they come from. Clint met quite a few people he knew. They enjoyed trading stories.

After lunch at Doña Amelia's he went to the bank to release funds to his good friend and nextdoor neighbor in Bocas Town, Judi Lum, for the projects they were working on, then went to the several places he liked in David. He enjoyed a delicious chicha at Disfrutas, then called Dave's (his nutty musician/botanist/author friend) lawyer to see what was happening with his case against some local would-be mafia types who had stolen his property. It seemed he was going to go public against the corruption in the courts. The lawyer was getting worried. Those people would have him killed if he got too close to catching them.

"What're you talking about? He has them cold, already!"

"He has to go through another judge who's just like the one he's after to have anything done. If one falls, several of them will fall. That's why they keep closing investigations on an excuse of insufficient evidence."

"He has contracts in Spanish. He didn't speak Spanish when they were registered. It says on the face of the first one that he speaks, reads and understands Spanish perfectly. He proved he didn't know more than a few words when he supposedly signed them. The notary who made them lost his license because of this case. The law here is clear that such contracts constitute fraud.

"He doesn't have sufficient evidence? Those contracts in Spanish are fraud – by definition – here!"

"That have to be acted upon by those judges," he replied, pointedly. "It is something that I hope he can slow down a little. I think it is not possible to stop it."

They discussed it a bit, then Clint went to the Costa Rica to change for dinner. He went to La

Tipica for the breaded shrimp. Tula was inland, meaning he didn't get much seafood there. He called his wife, Tyna, and spoke with her and their son, Nito for almost an hour. He was fortunate that there was a signal. Most times there was none in the area, even the direct satellite cell phones they used. They were his one concession to what was jokingly referred to as modern civilization.

He went to Peter's for a beer, then to Sasa, then to Sandy's, then to the Cantina Parque. He knew many of the regular clients of those four places. Around midnight he went back to the pensión. It had been a pleasant night.

In the morning he bought the rest of the things he needed and took it all to the terminal to have it put on the bus. He would leave at nine for Soloy. He would be back home in Tula tomorrow afternoon.

He used the time before the bus left to catch up on what was happening in the area. It seemed that some gringo was dead. He'd been hit over the head with a rock and had died of a fractured skull. He'd never regained consciousness. The theory was that someone tried to rob him and hit too hard. They must have been scared off because he had more than four thousand dollars in cash on him when he was found.

It didn't seem likely. Clint asked who the victim

was.

"A man from Tampa, Florida, in the states. His name was Calhoun. He had just won a lot of money gambling. Somebody saw him get paid off and tried to get the money."

Calhoun? Playing poker with Danny Betts, won big, then *he* gets offed? If it was Danny, he would have taken his money back. What was going on?

It wasn't his problem. Maybe Rodriguez set it up to get rid of Calhoun and make Danny the goat. It was how they operated.

Clint was in the first of the line to get on the bus. A heavy person wrapped up in loud cloth stepped in two people behind and went to sit next to him.

Oh, great! Some looney on a very long bus trip!

The person's hand came from the cloth. It was a pale-skinned hand that was wearing a large diamond ring that Clint had noted the day before.

"Betts? What the hell's going on!?"

"Wait until we're away from here! I should've listened to you! They were trying to force me to take ... I'll tell you when we're gone. You said you were going to Soloy. I waited by the bus loading until you came.

"It was horrible! I killed a man!"

Clint didn't say anything more until they were past Chiriqui. Betts sat beside him, glumly staring out the dirty side window. When they were approaching Boca del Morito, a small town where the bus turned to go to Soloy, Betts asked if he was going to have trouble because of the way he was dressed. Clint said they turned off before the check point. They would be in the comarca in a few minutes. He might have a bit of trouble there because very few gringos went to Soloy.

"Clint, what if Rodriguez has the police looking for me? I'm the only one who could have killed Calhoun."

"They were ... we'll get off in Boca del Morito and decide what you have to do."

When they turned Clint asked that his things on top of the bus be kept for him at the stop. He'd pick them up later. The driver and the door boy both knew him and would see that his stuff was okay. Before they got off the bus Betts took off the wraps. Andres, the door boy, said he wouldn't have let him get on the bus in David if he wasn't with Clint.

They got a refrescos at the bench where the woman had them in coolers, then went to sit under a tree past where they could be overheard.

"Well?"

Betts looked lost. He said, "It was a setup, just like you warned. They cheated, somehow, and I won a little, then lost a little, then the bets got higher and higher. I ran out of cash, but they said my credit was plenty good with them. I lost four thousand that I had and they got into me for six more. I said that was the limit. I couldn't keep playing.

"Rodriguez said I could do him a favor and the debt would be cancelled. I knew right then that you had been right. They cheated me and were going to make me do something.

"They had tried to get me to smoke some marijuana earlier. I'd said I didn't smoke since I was about seventeen or eighteen. Calhoun laughed and said he wasn't surprised. I looked like a country preacher. He bet they never searched me at the airports like they did everybody else, which was true. He said I could take a little package through when I go back next Saturday and they'd forget the bet.

"I said all bets were off the second they started cheating. I knew what they were doing. I just wanted to see what they were setting me up for.

"Calhoun got really nasty. I said maybe they'd like to discuss their little package with the police and they laughed at me. They said the package was from a judge and that they wouldn't even be asked the time of day by the police here.

"I said we'd see and was walking out when Rodriguez drew a pistol and said I wasn't going anywhere until we had a little discussion about obligations. I laughed in his face and went on out. Calhoun was right there behind me when I went out the door and tripped me. I went down, but I know how to roll and come right back up. I grabbed a rock about the size of a grapefruit and smacked him with it when he came at me. I don't know if I wanted to kill him, but I did. Rodriguez had stayed inside – see, we had three others in the game. They pulled that when they followed me to the pisser and nobody was around.

"Rodriguez called just before Calhoun charged me that Calhoun was to bring me back inside as soon as I saw reason and went on back to the game room.

"I smacked him with the rock and ran. I hid out and was terrified that the police would grab me and that they did have a judge to back them and I'd end up in some hellhole prison here for the rest of my life. I remembered that you had told us you were going to Soloy today. I used my Visa for some cash at the ATM and bought some cloth at that place down by the park that sells it. I waited until you came. Here I am."

"Rodriguez isn't going to say a word about you. A body means you could go to Panamá City and the judge here would be in deep doo-doo. They can buy a judge or two in David. It's common knowledge that some of them and some of the fiscaliá people are totally corrupt. It would bring too much attention to certain reporters who don't like most of the present administration about the rampant corruption they could get a feather or two for exposing.

"What Rodriguez has to do now is find a cover or get out before he can be exposed. It's going down to cover your own ass. That bunch have no morals, certainly no loyalty. Whatever, it will be fast. We can stay at a friend's place just three kilometers from here. Two days. We'll have an idea what you'll have to do by then. They'll definitely come after you if Rodriguez stays. If he goes, you won't even be mentioned except maybe by the other poker players there. You apparently weren't. There would have been some kind of search for you."

"They probably thought I'd left half an hour earlier. Rodriguez and Calhoun were always hearty and joking while we were around them."

"We wait and see. Come on. We can walk to Guillermo's place and nobody will know where we are in case anyone comes looking for you."

"How would they know I came here?"

"Rodriguez knows you met me?"

"I don't know. Maybe. We talked about a lot of things. Just chatter."

They strolled casually away. They didn't get any attention anyone would note, but Clint knew that several he knew would see him. They would also know not to say anything. If Clint didn't want to be seen, Clint wasn't seen.

They went to Guillermo's, where they were warmly welcomed. Clint explained that Betts had to be someone that no one had seen anywhere and who no one had ever met.

It was about two thirty when Clint's cellular buzzed. He looked at the caller ID and saw it was Privado.

"Habla!" he said into the phone.

"Clint Faraday? You don't know me. I'm Mike, Miguel, a friend of Danny Betts. He said to call you if there was an emergency and you'd pass him to me.

"Can I speak with him? Is he close enough, or should I call back later?"

"Danny Betts? Who the hell is Danny Betts? Why would he even have my number to give to anyone?"

Rodriguez rang off. Betts raised an eyebrow at Clint.

"Rodriguez is trying to find you. He plans on staying. You have to be silenced. You must have mentioned me. He's checking anyone he can find who you mentioned."

"I didn't have your number to give him! How did he get it?"

"A lot of people in David have my number. The police have it. If he has someone bought at the fiscalia it would take ten seconds."

"What should I do?"

"We'll go on to Soloy. I'll get you a place there where no one will mention ever having heard of you. I'll do a little private investigation of Miguel Rodriguez and what he's doing here. Maybe we can expose a corrupt judge in the process. If not, you'll have to lay low for a few weeks until they give it up. They'll figure you won't say anything if you didn't already."

They stayed the night at Guillermo's place and walked back to Boca del Morito. The bus was there loading passengers for David. The door boy saw Clint and called him over.

"Clint, a policeman came to me last night and asked if you had a friend with you and if you came to Soloy. I said that you always came to

Soloy alone unless you are with your wife and child. No one came there with you. Nobody got off in Soloy or anywhere else in the comarca who I don't know. It was true. You stopped off here."

"Thanks, Andres. A corrupt cop is trying to find him to shut him up about an illegal deal. If anyone thinks to ask if anyone you didn't know got off before here ... there were those three people who got off in Chiriqui near the university?"

"It will be true. The only ones I didn't know got off there. The dishonest police officer can spend days looking for someone who is there or who took the bus from there to Gualaca or Chorcha or somewhere."

They chatted a bit more. Clint asked Andres to carefully note anyone who asked about him or his friend in David.

They waited until the bus was gone for Clint to get them a ride with a friend who had vegetables from the comarca he had sent to David on the bus. They were in Soloy in two and a half hours. Clint arranged for his supplies to get to Quebrada Tula and settled Betts in a place in town where no one will ever have heard of him or seen him.

Clint called Tyna and talked for almost an hour. Nito had made friends with a couple of boys his age and they had gone to the river to swim. One boy had an older brother, eight years old, who would be there to be sure they were safe in the water and that no snakes or whatever else would bother them.

Clint was amazed at himself to not be too seriously concerned that his less than two year old son was going swimming and was wandering around the jungle with two others his age and only an eight year old boy was there with them. At eight, Indio children were responsible. They had a place in the family and community. In the US he wouldn't let his kid go anywhere with anyone until he was fourteen or fifteen and they would have to have adult supervision even at that age.

Sure, there were a very few perverts and worse among the Indios, the same as anywhere else, but the fact the older boy was there and there were three of them meant there would be no problems. In addition, it was well enough known that to try anything with Clint Faraday's child would mean a slow and horrible death. Clint had come around to the Indio way of thinking about that. An adult was anyone over twelve years of age. Less than that, you are a child. No one messes with a child. Period. Ever. Adults did what they wanted, which was going to be hard on him when his son was twelve and ready to make his own decisions.

That was years away. He didn't see where it had done any harm to any indigeno, even those in the towns where they were exposed to everything.

What a time to be thinking of that!

He finally rang off and told Betts he was going to David to see if he could learn anything about what was going on.

"It's a drug deal, right?" Betts asked.

"To tell the truth, I don't think so. A package you could carry that was small enough to carry that way wouldn't be drugs. It would have to be something that wouldn't draw any attention."

"I was thinking along those lines. For it to make a ten thousand dollar loss part of the expense says it was something else."

"And!" Clint pointed out. "It's something that's valuable enough that Miguel Rodriguez stayed here under the circumstances. I don't have a clue, but I have some people to check."

They made plans, mainly to stay out of sight, then Clint caught a ride on a delivery truck to Boca del Morito where he could catch a number of buses for David.

Clint checked into the Toledo Hotel. He could go anywhere he wanted from there and wasn't so well known as at the Costa Rica or Alcalá or such. He didn't think he would need a disguise, but that was an option. He used them at times. He was good at it.

Betts had given him information about what places they had been and who else had been there who he knew at all. Rodriguez was staying at the Ciudad de David. He went to the restaurant there. He was about to be seated when he thought of something and told the waiter he would be back later.

Rodriguez knew him by sight. He'd met him in Tampa some years ago and might have seen him here. He would need that disguise.

The somewhat bullish man with the salt and pepper short military-style haircut dressed in camouflage fatigues and military boots with a tee shirt with "Vietnam Vet" on the front marched to a chair at a table near the back in the Ciudad de David Restaurant amid stares. The waiter came over to ask what he wanted.

"This is a restaurant?" he said, a bit loudly. "I want a damned menu! Why the hell else would I be here?"

The boy handed him the menu and walked off. The man shook his head and mumbled something nasty. He read over the menu and snapped his fingers. The boy came back with his pad and stood there.

"T-bone, rare. Mashed potatoes. Green salad. Iced tea."

The boy walked off. The man looked around. A woman at the next table called the waiter over and asked that she and her friend be moved to a better location.

"You have the freedom where you can come here and move to another table because people like me were fighting for your rights!" the man snapped.

"Really? You *lost* in Vietnam, if I recall?" she said and followed the waiter to a table across the restaurant.

"Bitch!" he snapped.

The woman's friend came to stand over Clint. "You'll apologize to the lady for that! Now!" he demanded.

"And if I don't?"

"Then you will be arrested and will go to prison

for slander," the waiter said. "Your speech and actions tell me you would be at home there! Be so kind as to remove yourself from the premises – after apologizing to the lady."

The friend was still there. He wasn't nearly so big as Clint, but Clint knew that he would take a beating by challenging the person who had just insulted his friend. Then Clint would go to jail for ten different charges. He was playing the misfit all-bluff character, so mumbled that he apologized for his remarks.

The man and his lady friend walked away. The waiter pointed to the door.

Rodriguez was two tables away. He stood as Clint headed for the door and came to say, "A moment?"

"I said I was sorry! I get crazy sometimes! I was wrong and know it or I would've knocked that swishy bastard on his ass!"

"Where are you from?" Rodriguez asked.

"America! Chicago, Illinois!"

"I see. I can guess what part. Where were you raised? You don't sound Chicago."

"Around. Houston, L. A., The Apple. Around."

"Military brat?"

"Yeah. It shows, huh?"

"And you weren't in Vietnam."

Clint stared hard at him for a few seconds, then

shrugged and grinned. "No. Section eight. After boot. Paris Island."

"You don't and can't fit here. I don't know how you got here. They wouldn't let you on a plane?"

"They don't give me any shit. I want to get on, I give them the shiv and anything else I might be carrying. They read my pass from D.C. and don't ask questions. According to the pass I'm airport security. Pops got me that. They say anything I'm undercover."

"Oh? You mean they let you just stroll onto an international flight and don't even check to see if you gave them everything?"

"They got the detectors. I don't carry anything except for clothes and shit."

"I'm Mike Rodriguez. I have a little problem I want to get checked out. I work for international security myself, but it's for real.

"There are some people we have to get goods on. We have to find out how they're getting some things into the states. You should be in a position where we find out."

"Drugs? Just put them in something for deck cargo on a boat. You don't use planes for that shit anymore."

"I couldn't care less about drugs. That's another department.

"What's your name? I think maybe you can help

us. You'll also make a decent bundle because the department will pay you ten thousand dollars if you can get stuff through and can show them how and keep mum about it."

"William Arnold Rhamer! Call me War. I could use a little stash of cash. I'm down to next to nothing. A couple trips like that and I can bum around another couple of years. A bum is all I'm really good for."

"Well, good! I'm in room ... here." He wrote some things on a business card and handed it to Clint. "I'll be there about one. I have a date that will take until then."

"What kind of stuff is it?"

"I'll explain later. You won't be carrying the real thing. Even we wouldn't take that chance!"

"Oh? C-four and better? Coming through places like here from Iran?"

"Not Iran, but that kind of thing. We have to stop it! We're afraid they're going to smuggle in enough stuff to make a dirty nuclear!"

"I'm in for that! See you at one fifteen!" He saluted and walked off.

He wondered what he would really be expected to deliver. He was about to make a challenge, but he'd been involved in two things that had to do with nuclears. One was about uranium from right here in Panamá.

He'd know after one o'clock. He wondered if he should be wired, but thought better of it. If they were into anything like that, he would be checked.

He could do one thing. He grinned to himself.

He went to La Tipica and had a good breaded shrimp dinner, then to Peter's, at the Hotel Iris. He was avoided quite efficiently there, so went to the Cantina Parque, where a Panamanian came to stand by him and say, "SEALS. Quatros años. San Diego."

"If you were in the SEALS, the last fucking thing you'd do is say so. You'd be also speaking English to me, shithead. Take a hike!"

"Que?"

"Vete!" He looked confused and started to say something. Clint stood and said, "Want to see what happens to your stupid face with someone who *has* the training?"

He turned and left. The barmaid grinned and rolled her eyes. He grinned back.

A big black man at the end of the bar came to say, "I was in the Navy in the US, but I wasn't any SEAL or anything else. I was a swabby.

"That guy always pulls that act when a gringo comes in. I don't think he fools anyone. He's got a problem."

"You can look at me and know I have a big problem, but I don't claim any of that shit. I was in, then I was out. Big fucking deal. It's a lot easier if I look like some kind of shell-shocked nutcase."

"You're one thing most of the type aren't! Honest!"

They chatted for awhile. Clint walked around awhile, then headed for the Ciudad de David.

Clint knocked on the door. Rodriguez answered and waved him in. The black from the Cantina Parque was sitting there with a big grin.

"You can see I had you checked. I'm glad to say you checked out very well. You've met Luis.

"I have one question, though. It puzzles me.

"Why do you do so many things that will draw attention to yourself?"

"Because people's attention span is short. Act like you want attention, they lose interest."

He laughed. "That's why they don't bother you much at airports. The very last thing anyone who was up to anything would do is draw attention to themselves! Very clever! You also do it in such a way that they have to believe you're a super-patriotic loon!"

"I am patriotic. Just not extreme."

They chatted for a few minutes. Clint's phone buzzed at just the wrong moment. He answered and said he was busy. Call in the morning. It was Tyna. She would know he was in a place where he couldn't talk. It did give him an excellent opportunity to put a part of his plan into action.

He put the Blackberry back into his pocket and said, "So? What's it about? I take it somebody's trying to get stuff into the states, but don't see why the easier ways, like inside large auto parts or such as deck cargo aren't used. I can take a couple of pounds on as hand luggage. A couple tons could be sent as deck cargo."

"The nuclear thing. Deck cargos are checked for radiation. Hand luggage isn't."

"So I'm supposed to carry a lot of radioactive crap around with me? For ten grand? You're as nuts as I act!"

"You won't be carrying radioactives. We aren't about to actually send any such thing on a plane!" Rodriguez cried. "They can get by with very little leakage, but detectable. We think they simply put a couple of those old wristwatches with glow-in-the-dark radium hands in their luggage. That will be found if it's checked and will explain the leakage."

"It's not radioactives," Luis said. "It's other things that would serve the same purpose. Raise havoc in a large segment of the public."

"Like ricin? Bubonic plague?"

"There are worse things. You won't carry even that stuff," Rodriguez answered. It sounded a little stiff and rehearsed. He had come up with a story since meeting "War" in the restaurant. "It goes by plane because it has what you'd call a short shelf life. They haven't taken any in yet, but they've made what looks like practice runs. We have to know what they plan. How they'll carry it.

"Part is, of course, to make several trips so they're known at the airports."

"Yeah. Then the inspector says, 'Oh, hi, Lola! Go on through! We know you're alright!' Even a stewardess could get away with it, but I know damned well you'd catch onto them fast!" Clint replied. "So. How's it going to go down?"

"We give you a little box like we estimate they would use. We put something like a knick-knack you buy in it. It's the kind of thing that will be checked. It just doesn't have to be checked so close. All you have to do is prove to my superiors how easy it is. You give them the box after you get through, they give you ten grand and say where and when to meet for the next assignment to deliver. If it's not checked, there's a lax spot in the movement that we have to close! You get the ten grand for any you get through. You get five if you can't get it through."

"You can work that with any tourist."

"They check the type they think we'd use. They take one look at you and your method works. It points something out to them!"

"My method?"

"Be so obvious it couldn't be you," Luis said. "You can't believe how stupid some of the top people in this can be. Political appointees, but we have to do what we can. If we can get two or three through where they don't catch you we can threaten to go public if they don't stop it."

Clint nodded. He said he saw some of that a few years ago. News reporters setting things up that were so obvious it was pathetic and not being caught.

They talked for awhile longer. Clint would have his first package ready for his planned return to the states. He told them next Friday. That was one day ahead of when Betts was supposed to go. He soon went back to the Toledo.

He had the Blackberry recording the whole thing since Tyna's call. He'd turned the recorder on when he put the phone back into his pocket. He managed to turn around with it in his hand so the video would get a good part of it before it went into his pocket. He would download it to his computer and clear the memory on the phone of that segment.

He did that, put the phone on the charger, and went to bed. Next would be getting the box and finding what was really in it. That this would be the real whatever it was was plain enough.

A knick-knack? How would they work that?

Would it be something hidden inside or the thing itself?

In the morning he went carefully through the stuff on the comp. The video managed to get good shots of Luis and Rodriguez and a number of things around the room. There were various items there. On the bed was a plastic sack with a few items of the type tourists buy. Clint supposed whatever he was to deliver would be in one of those four boxes. He studied them as closely as he could. Typical things.

Why have a spray can of clear acrylic sealer? That didn't seem to fit anything! Anything that didn't fit could be an important clue.

The voices had come through very well. There would be no problem with that part.

Okay. He had six days. He would concentrate on finding what he could about Luis.

He called Tonio and said to quietly find what he could. He was probably staying at the Ciudad de David and was as obviously not Panamanian. His passport might tell them something.

Six days. He called Rodriguez and said he was going to go to Puerto Armuelles or something and would be back Friday morning. He went to a friend near the airport as himself and hired a chopper to take him to Quebrada Tula and his family. He would be flown back Friday morning.

It was a good thing he'd made so much on some of his cases. The chopper both ways cost twelve hundred bucks!

He thought and arranged that the chopper come for him Thursday afternoon. It might be a good idea to talk with Tonio, then arrange to be back in town by eleven or so to call Rodriguez to say he was back.

Nito and Clint went swimming with Nito's new friends. The older brother, Orlando, was a serious type who soon had warmed to Clint as he already had to Tyna. There were two boys and two girls in their very early teens there who got along very well. They teased the way teenagers teased. One of them said he didn't know whether he wanted to screw his girlfriend or Orlando, who was really handsome. Orlando said he didn't think he'd like that. Clint knew how it was only partly a joke, but Orlando said no, so that was that.

Back in the states he would have gone into a rage if some teenage boy tried to seduce an eight year old boy. Here it only amused him.

Not on that tack again! Was it because he knew perfectly damned well Nito would one day be getting such propositions? Probably before he was eight?

Orlando was a good person to have at such

times. He would teach his brother and Nito and friends that all they had to do was say, "No." It was the way. He wondered if any boy reached twelve who hadn't been seduced before. They knew whether they liked it or not.

Would it bother him? It was seduction, not rape. He knew what he would do if it was rape.

He didn't really know. He remembered sleeping wrapped up together with several Indio men and how he wondered what would happen if it came up. It hadn't come up. He knew in one instance that he wouldn't have refused.

Well, that would come in its own time. For Nito and for him.

The rest of the five days were perfect as that had been. He had asked Tyna about the things he was considering at the swimming hole. She said boys will be boys and girls will be girls. It hadn't changed in the past million years and wouldn't change in the next. She was surprised that he hadn't ever experimented when he was young. He tried to tell her about the difference in the states and here. She said there wasn't any real difference. She couldn't understand how people could raise children in a way that when things happened that almost always did happen they would be made to feel they had done something horrible, even when it wasn't their doing. How could anyone be that stupid? It was like that stupidity when a friend had tried to get her to become a catholic. She was supposed to believe she was a sinner when she was born, before she even had the ability to have a thought?

"Nito is going to get screwed and he'll probably do a bit of screwing himself with his friends. You can't pretend it doesn't happen. Here, you know that it will happen. It happened to all your friends and your father and uncles and everyone else in your family but you. It didn't hurt any of them so why think it's going to hurt Nito? Maybe if it had happened to you you wouldn't even think about it. I agree that we're talking about being seduced. Rape? That isn't even thinkable. That's violating your body. It shouldn't be tolerated under any circumstances. By anyone at any age.

"I think when a bunch of you get drunk and start joking and you get held down and screwed it isn't rape. You were there and doing the same thing and you knew it would happen. Maybe you hoped you would be on the other end of the stick, but that's the bet you placed and you knew it. That's just competition. Even when you end up the one screwed you have to admit that it was a lot of fun.

"Not you! I'm talking about normal people."

"You're saying I'm not normal?"

"Of course you're not! I couldn't picture living

with a normal person! Yuck!"

They teased and played. They ended up in bed, but they both were aiming for that from the first. It was a great life here in paradise. Tyna was a fantastic woman. Come to think of it, Nito was one fantastic kid! So were his friends, even the boy who wanted to seduce Orlando.

Clint and Tyna were laying cuddled close in exhaustion when Nito came in. He climbed into the bed with them. It was two hours later when they all woke up. Esteban, a close neighbor, had called from out front. Nito told Tyna and Clint to put on some clothes and went to tell Esteban to come on inside. He was stark naked, but said he was a little kid. Nobody expected him to wear clothes.

Clint laughed and held Tyna. "God, I love you! I love Nito, I love this place, I love my people, I love life!

"I think I'll tell Tonio to grab their package and see what's going on. I don't want to go back there again!"

"Oh, you'll go. You're caught in two different worlds. Neither is enough, but together they are."

"I think you've got it. I haven't yet, but you have."

If Esteban hadn't been sitting on the porch they would have gotten into teasing again. They got up and threw on some clothes and went out. Tyna fixed some chicha and they talked until almost dark, then they went to the river to bathe.

Thursday morning the chopper came at ten as promised. Clint was ready. He said he'd be back as soon as he could. Tyna was right when she said he would never be happy in either of his worlds exclusively.

He went to the Hotel Madrid this time. He put on the disguise before he left the chopper airport. He called Tonio, who said Luis Carter was just a guy who worked for a company that owned several bars and nightclubs in the Tampa Bay area. He didn't have a bad reputation, but it was nowhere near perfect, either. He wasn't directly accused of anything, but he kept company with some very bad-news people.

He waited to call Rodriguez until ten thirty and arranged to meet them in the morning before the flight to learn who to contact in Miami after he got through airport security and customs offices. He then went to several places before turning in. He wondered again what they were going to give him to deliver that was worth their staying silent when one of them was killed and ten thousand for delivery after that had taken the chances they took to stay there.

He did get into a conversation with a man who

was, if you knew the signs, working for the CIA or Interpol or something. He had run across such people at times before and saw right away they weren't interested in him.

He went to the Madrid and to bed.

He went to breakfast as soon as a place was open. He walked around a bit. No one was about that early except people who were catching the early buses to work or whatever. He then went to the Ciudad de David to meet with Rodriguez. Luis came to them a few minutes later, carrying a backpack. He said they would check through their luggage together. He was going to Tucumen to draw some attention when they were being checked through for the direct flight to Miami. It would be just enough to make them detain him there. If anyone was expecting anything, he would be checked. Suspicion would only be on him, meaning War could breeze right on through.

Oh, great! He wasn't going to Miami!

"I've got tickets waiting in Panamá City. You do have your passport and the paper to let you get through?" Rodriguez asked. "I think there won't be any problems.

"You will meet a man at Miami International who will be carrying a sign that says 'Oliver B. Smith.' You will walk past him and manage to check your wristwatch right in front of him and

look up to the big clock on the wall there. Go to
the taxi stand and the man will get a taxi for you.
You will take the package to meet another man,
who will give you ten thousand dollars in cash —
if you manage to get through.

"That's it! Come back here in a day or two and
we can arrange for the next one."

Clint nodded and shook his hand. He said he
wanted some breakfast. They could join him. It
was more than an hour for the flight to PMA.
They said they had to make some arrangements.
They would meet him when he went through
security to give him the package, which he would
put in his suitcase like it was gifts for children or
girlfriends or something. There would be a form
receipt in the package that would mean he would
have to pay about fifteen dollars import. Luis
would give him a hundred dollars to cover such
expenses.

He got a call from Rodriguez, who said his flight
was now on another airline an hour later.

"We think the bigshots will figure we're setting
something up and will be waiting to triumphantly
grab you. You won't be on that flight. They're a
little slow and will think we've moved it ahead,
not back," Luis explained. "You don't mind, do
you?"

"It's all the same to me," Clint answered. "I just

want to get it done so I can get back here. I really liked Puerto Armuelles. I met a twenty six year old girl from Michigan who was staying with friends out toward the oil pipeline terminal and we had a hell of a time."

"Oh. Your phone wasn't answered," Rodriguez said. Clint had noted the incoming calls and had deliberately not answered.

"I left it at her place. It was almost discharged when I remembered it. I did see where I had a few missed calls."

As soon as he was away from them he called Tonio and explained what was going on. Tonio would manage to have him handed the necessary papers as soon as they arrived. If Luis was going to cause a diversion, it would be perfect. Things would be arranged at Tucumen and ready to go. He would call the embassy in Miami and tell them to expect Clint and to cooperate. They would learn who they contacted in Miami, this way.

Clint called Tyna and explained. She laughed. She said that was about what could be expected. Take the greatest care. She didn't want to have to break in a new husband.

He met Luis in the baggage check line. He was not to act as though they knew each other. Luis acted nervous and drew the attention of a guard, who made a call, then came to ask if anything was wrong.

"I'm a little afraid of airplanes is all. I took a tranquilizer five minutes ago, so it'll kick in soon. If it wasn't for this I'd really love my job."

Luis was four people ahead of him in the line. He watched when Clint gave the guard a paper. (Actually, the guard had a paper he acted as though he was handed by Clint.) The guard went to his supervisor, who said something. The guard came back, handed him the paper, along with a passport and some identification as a police expert working for the Panamanian government in international security, and passed him through. Luis was waiting in the waiting area and asked if that was the paper his father gave him to get him through.

"No. It was a form they gave me at Tucumen when I came in. Mine is in English. This one's in Spanish. She asked why it was from Continental and I'm taking Copa back. I said the person I'm watching booked on Copa. It was only natural they'd arrange for me to be on that flight.

"He said there were two very suspicious people. Maybe one was my quarry?

"I said it was possible. I couldn't tell anyone who I was watching."

Luis nodded. They got on the flight and arrived in Tocumen an hour later. Luis slipped Clint the package, about eight inches square and a little heavy. He put it in his carry-on. There were five twenty dollar bills in the tie-string he put in his pocket.

They were standing in the boarding line when two guards came to Luis and said to come with them. He winked at Clint and went with them. When the flight took off he hadn't returned.

Shit! Miami, here I come! Whoopee!

Miami was the usual hell to get through. When he got to customs he presented the package and papers from Tonio. They were expecting him.

They opened the package to find four boxes with huge jewels in heavy silver settings. Two emeralds, a ruby and a diamond. The boxes had little "Made in Taiwan" stickers. The stones looked almost real. There was just a hint too little refraction and one had a slight scratch that showed a flash when turned at an angle. The four agents there looked at each other and shrugged.

"I guess this is a test to see if you can get through."

Clint remembered the clear acrylic paint spray can and smirked. "I'd say you have about six million bucks worth of antique pirate treasure there. We found some of it on a case."

He explained about the findings and that most of the relics had disappeared within a month. They carefully photographed the jewels from all angles. Clint showed the stones underneath by scraping off a very small spot of the acrylic paint that was sprayed there to reduce refraction. They discussed it and what they could do that wouldn't let on that they had found them. Clint said he could either fold and let them find the jewels or bluff it through long enough for them to find who was selling the items in the government.

He finally went to take the old duffle bag from the rack and head for the taxi stand. The man with the sign was there. Clint went through the ritual. It might have looked strange if anyone else had been watching for someone to check a wristwatch they weren't wearing, then the wall clock.

He went outside. The man with the sign came out behind him and asked if he could get a cab for him. He was about to say, "Okay!" when a man in a suit grabbed the guy and told Clint to stand right there. "FBI!"

Clint shrugged and stood there. There was no way an actual FBI agent would pull that kind of act, but he could thank TV for making a lot of people think they would.

"Do you know this man?" the supposed agent asked.

"No. Should I?"

"Don't get cute! Drop the bag!"

"Show me some ID, big bad FBI man!" Clint sat the bag down. Another man came up behind and opened the bag. Clint's back was to him. He was staring down the phony FBI agent. The man with the sign was staring wide-eyed. He started to say something and the agent snarled, "One word and you spend ninety days for resisting!"

He flipped open a case with a badge and card in it and flipped it shut before Clint could read it.

"Take it out of the case, Sir!" Clint said.

"I don't have time for this shit! You're about to get in over your head with me! I promise you'll regret it!"

Clint turned to the man with the sign. "He's a phony dickhead. Tell him to fuck the hell off." He nodded shortly to the phony agent and went to the waiting taxi. Clint got in and said to take him to a cheap nearby motel. One night here and he was gone! Miami was worse every time he came there!

The driver grinned and said, "Mr. Santiago's expecting you. How did you spot that turkey as a phony?"

"Experience. Lots and lots of experience."

They drove out toward Lauderdale, turned into a private road that was better maintained than the public roads, and to a big Spanish Rancho style house where Clint was ushered in to meet Juan Pablo Santiago V. Santiago was a slick slightly heavy man in his late fifties or early sixties. He didn't waste time with introductions. He held out his hand. Clint tossed the duffle bag to him. He went through it and said, "Well?"

Clint asked what was the matter.

"Where is it?"

"Right there on top! What do you mean?"

"It is not right there on top or anywhere else! Where is it!?"

Clint grabbed the bag. The package was gone.

"But...! I saw them put it in there! I had to pay forty seven dollars customs and they put it right there! It was right there! What the hell..?!

"Maybe your bosses weren't fooled by your test, but there's no way ... it was right there!"

"Gonzo! Get Raul in here! Now!"

"What is this? What are you setting me up for?" Clint demanded. "I only did what Rodriguez said! I don't know what's going on!"

"Wait. We'll see what happened. I won't accuse you of anything until I know."

"Gonzo" brought the very scared taxi driver in. Santiago asked if there was anytime anyone could have gotten to Clint's bag that he wouldn't know about.

"I don't think so. Maybe when the phony FBI guy grabbed Max."

"Phony FBI? Grabbed Max?"

"Yeah. At the terminal. Max was getting a cab for this guy here, me, and some phony FBI guy grabbed him and started yelling. This guy backed him down and told Max to tell the crud to fuck off. He was phony.

"Let's see. The FBI guy said something to this guy and this guy got in his face and said he had to show some ID and the FBI guy flashed a cardcase with a badge or something at him. He stood there and just stared ... hey! There was some other guy who came up behind! I couldn't see anything because the column was in the way! He could've done something!"

There was a lot of noise and the sign man came bursting in. He had a black eye and bloody nose.

"What? Fast!" Santiago demanded.

"There was this guy who said he was from the FBI...."

"We know that. What happened?"

"This guy here was in his face and looked like he was about to kick his stupid ass – the FBI guy, I mean – and some other suit came and took something out of this guy's bag! I tried to tell him, but the other one slugged me and I went down. When I got up everybody was gone!"

"Santiago, who – beside you, me, Luis and Rodriguez – knew about this?" Clint asked.

"Who, indeed?"

"Well, you know another thing to watch for. This test gave you some answers, even if they weren't what you were looking for. It's a good thing it was only cheap costume crap. There's somebody, probably the one you're buying from or something, who was setting you up."

"Who we're buying from? What did Rodriguez tell you?"

"I'm not stupid. His story didn't make any sense. I suppose you really have some jewels to get out of Panamá. They found a lot of pirate shit a couple of years ago that was worth hundreds of millions. It would be that. A friend said it had almost all evaporated. Or something."

"What would you say if I told you those you brought weren't phony."

Clint looked thoughtful. "Really?"

"Seven point four million."

"Nah-ah! I saw them in the customs office. They were damned good, but you could tell they were phony. Real jewels will catch that kind of light and blind you! They just sparkled a lot."

"We know a way to hide the refraction."

"I'll be goddamned!"

"I think you're not ... maybe you'd like a job? Maybe you can make the ten grand and a lot more?"

"What's the deal? I could use some income."

"We won't tell the Mr. Rodriguez type this didn't go down exactly as planned. You will go back to Panamá and will let them arrange the next shipment. If they don't know about this, their supplier, as you suggested, will be the one we have to handle. If they do know about it, we have yet another answer, don't we?"

"Hard to argue."

"Let's make a little plan of our own. I always considered that we may lose a shipment or two. This only means we have to make certain it doesn't happen again. As you can see by looking around here, seven or eight million don't unduly bother me.

"I will pay you two million dollars to find who is really behind this. Deal?"

"Deal! I'll need a little for operating expenses. A few hundred."

"You were to receive ten thousand dollars to deliver the package or five if you didn't. You didn't. I owe you five thousand dollars." He opened his desk drawer and tossed Clint a packet of fifty hundred dollar bills. There were two in the drawer. That will be more than I need. I hope to collect two million dollars from you within, say, ten days?"

"If it takes that little, you get a bonus on top of it!" They shook hands and Santiago told the taxi driver to take Clint to the hotel.

"Take me to the airport first. I want to book a flight back as quick as I can!"

He went out. The bluff had worked – so far!

Clint got off the plane and stretched. He went through customs, the papers letting him pass right through. Luis was waiting at the baggage checkout after customs

"That was fast!"

"Yeah. I got the same old guy who checked me through yesterday. He asked what happened with the gifts and I told him I got a piece of ass and promises for three more. Cheaper than hookers, but they are. Who cares?"

He laughed. "We can go meet Mike for dinner. I guess it was too early for it on the plane."

"Yeah. By half an hour! Am I glad to be back! You can have Miami!"

They went to a good restaurant. Clint acted like he had been offered pay to deliver a package, he delivered the package, he got paid. Next job?

Rodriguez said they would go back to David. He had to check with people there to see if there were rumblings yet. That would mean the higher-ups had tumbled that something was up. They would have to be more careful in the future. Clint said he could use a few days to travel around. He really liked the Chiriqui area. Particularly Puerto Armuelles on the Pacific side and Bocas on the Caribbean side.

They went to David on the morning flight and separated at the airport. Clint went to the chopper field when he was certain they were gone. He headed for Quebrada Tula and his family home. Rodriguez would call as soon as he had something set up. Probably a week or ten days. He would be back in David before then. He wanted a few days with Tyna and Nito. He would have to figure when whoever was selling the articles to Rodriguez would be around to find. He had a few ideas. Tonio would be watching for a certain type to come there.

Six days. Tonio had called and said one of the type Clint asked about was going to be in David for two or three days. He was an ex-governor of a province toward Colón who had not sought the post after he was accused of corruption (more than is the norm). Jaime Jimenez Lopez. He was noted when he came through the Tolé checkpoint half an hour ago. He was driving a black '78 Lincoln continental.

Cripes! That old four sixty ate gas like it was going out of style in the seventies! He has to be doing something to be able to afford to drive it down the street, much less all the way from Colón! Clint thought.

He told Tyna the case was calling and he had to go. He called the chopper and put on his disguise. He was in David about the time Jimenez arrived. He checked into the Riviera this time. He was just getting settled in when he got the call from Rodriguez that he could plan another trip for Tuesday. He said he'd be ready. He was already back in David. He kind of liked Aguadulce.

So. Jimenez was it! How could he set it up to where the police could tag him? He damned well knew who to bribe and had the funds!

Clint called Tonio to discuss how to handle things. They would have to wait to see what kind of opportunity would arise. They knew there was to be a transfer. The time to act was while it was being made.

"Rodriguez called on Nando Ramirez, a pawnbroker who has one hell of a lot of money more than he can account for. I think he's involved. He's probably the contact man for Jimenez."

Clint thought for a minute, then called the ultra-private number Santiago had given him. "Name Nando Ramirez mean anything to you?"

A slight pause. "He handles the cash transfers. For me."

"Anybody else who knows what's going down

that you didn't bother to tell me about?"

"No. I never considered him. He it?"

"I don't think so. Rodriguez went to see him."

"I think I can trust him."

"You thought you could trust all of them."

"True. Point taken. No one seems to know too much?"

"Not sure. There's one more I have to check out. It's looking like someone there in Miami is behind something."

"I don't see how, but I'll check it out ten ways from Sunday."

"The one you're selling to ask any questions?"

"I'm not selling. I'm keeping the rocks because jewels of that type don't lose value when the economy crashes – like it'll do any day."

"Yeah. I'm buying gold with what I get."

"Good. It'll retain a lot of it's value. I figured you're a lot smarter than you let on."

"I try to stay out of sight. If you checked on me through the airline you didn't get anything. The special agent schtick means nobody saw me or knows who the hell you're asking about."

"Which means you actually are."

"Was. I'm dead. There's no record of when the papers are used. They won't find out until I really am dead. They can dig me up and prosecute my remains."

He laughed. "I think you keep any deal you make. It keeps you dead without really being dead."

"I do what I set out to do. I said I would find who's behind this crap. That's exactly what I'll do. I'll let you know when I'm sure. I just think I know right now. I also don't make mistakes about identifying people. Get the wrong one and my cover just went over the falls."

"You think you know?"

"A politician, but that would be so easy to figure it doesn't count. Actually, a crooked ex-politician. He was bounced."

"It would seem Rodriguez would know who it is in that case. I guess Nando wants to be sure we don't drop him from the chain."

"Rodriguez and Luis both know, I think.

"Maybe not. That could be why I found that Nando. Rodriguez went straight to him after I got back."

"Check it out! If they know, it was them who set me up!"

"Oh, I'll check out a lot of things. That's one of them!"

He hung up after another minute and looked at Tonio. "When did Rodriguez go to Nando's?"

"Day before yesterday. Four o'clock PM."

"I'll be damned! Jimenez was already on the way

here! Maybe they *are* setting Santiago up!"

"It would be all of them, then?"

"Or maybe a combination. Was Luis with Rodriguez when he went to Nando's?"

"No."

Clint nodded and sighed. "This is going to get damned hairy I'm very much afraid! I wonder what they'll pull ... and I think I know! Guess who's supposed to get set up next!"

"Ah! *You!*"

"We'll have a little surprise waiting for them." He called Santiago again.

"Okay, now I'll level all the way with you. I work with the Panamanian government. We wanted to know who grabbed the treasure and exactly how it was handled. We now know.

"Listen, Mr. Santiago. Three people are setting this up. I'm to be the next goat. They don't know we got the first shipment. I'll arrange for you to keep that if you'll help us with this. I think I know what they plan. That way Panamá won't lose this treasure. I'm sure not much has been moved yet.

"You can warn them, but then there won't be anymore going out and you wouldn't get your investment back."

"Sounds like fun! What do you want me to do?"

They spent more than an hour discussing what they would do. It was mostly reacting to what

Rodriguez and company did. When they were through Clint went around the town as before. He met Luis at Sasa's and they chatted. Luis asked why he'd gone to the police station.

"That head cop, Tonio, is one smart dude! He had me noted when I gave them the papers at the airport and wants to know what's going down. He doesn't want to arrest another officer of the law."

Luis studied him a minute. "I like you. You're honest and ten times as savvy as you let on. You know what we're doing, don't you?"

"More or less. I think they're keeping things from you. You're friends with Santiago?"

"In a way. He helped my family a few years ago when everything seemed hopeless and I started getting in with that gangster crowd in Tampa. He kept me out of serious trouble. I owe him."

"Do you know what they plan?"

"Who?"

"Rodriguez and Nando and Jimenez."

"Nando? Jimenez?"

"They're setting Santiago up. That means they set me up. They planned to rip him off all the way."

"Are you sure?" He was staring intensely into Clint's eyes.

"Ninety five percent."

"I wish I could get in touch with Santiago. I

would warn him.”

Clint took out his phone and called. Santiago answered. He said Luis wasn’t involved and wanted to warn him about Rodriguez. He handed the phone to Luis, who chatted a few minutes, then handed the phone back.

“Luis will be working for me under your orders. You can trust him. I know.”

“Good! I think I know what they plan. You already sent the money for the next shipment?”

“Ah! Yes. This is the big one, nine million. It will be enough that they can give their excuses not to do more. I won’t get any next shipment?”

“I think you’ll get it. I’ll bring it, but it won’t get to you.”

“So. This time they *will* set you up?”

“That, or ... something else they can blame on me.”

“Well, surprise, surprise!”

“Uh-huh!”

Santiago chatted with Clint a minute, then with Luis. Luis asked what he was to do.

“Act like you’re still on the outside and don’t know from nothin’. We have to see what they plan.”

“Will they let me in on it? *He*. Rodriguez is the one I know.”

“I don’t think so, but you can see what’s going

on."

"Because they won't expect me to be looking."

"Dju godt it!"

They forgot about the intrigues and had a fun evening. Clint set Luis up with a girl he knew and went back to the hotel alone at a little after midnight.

In the morning Rodriguez called and said he was moving the shipment date up. Tomorrow at nine. Be at the airport. They would do the same thing as before.

"No. Luis causing a disturbance will just get them suspicious of me. I'm there and talking with him, which I'm sure a couple noticed, then he gets detained again. Won't work."

"They won't check me. I'll manage to get the same baggage checker."

Rodriguez sounded thoughtful. "I guess you're right. You can go on your own this time. It'll all be up to you.

"You realize that you have to take the blame if anything goes wrong? No one will be there to see that you handled it correctly?"

"Okay by me. It's a gravy run." *So. I'll be to blame. Exactly what you were shooting for! Aren't you lucky!*

They talked for a few minutes, then Rodriguez rung off. The phone was buzzing again almost immediately. "I meant to ask if you saw Luis last night. He never came back to the hotel."

"I introduced him to a lady. He probably spent the night with her."

"Oh. Thanks."

Clint went for breakfast and to walk around the parque awhile, then spent some time chatting with people he'd met. He'd spotted the amateur who was keeping an eye on him right away and managed to go into Romero's and immediately out the back door. The follower was lounging on the light pole across the street in front of the joyeria. The other one he'd seen a few times too many had the sense to come inside the store, at least.

Not that it mattered. The ruse worked on him as well. A pause of thirty seconds was more than enough. The guy would search in the feriteria and store for a few minutes, then realize he had been outmaneuvered. Clint wondered what his excuse would be. Maybe he'd cover and not report it.

Clint went to set things up with Tonio.

The rest of the day was just lazing around and meeting people. He picked up both tails again at the parque.

Clint ate a good meal at the Alcalá and went back to the hotel early, where he sacked out for a restful night, was up at dawn, as usual, and had a good breakfast. He saw his tail from last night across from the hotel, so managed to move across the parking lot between cars and then behind shrubbery to the side road. The other one was on the corner where he could see down the side road. Clint waited until a bus turned in front of him, blocking his view, and dodged across to where the wall by a shop would hide him. He got a taxi on the next corner back and went to La Tipica, then walked the two blocks to the police station. He spent fifteen minutes discussing options with Tonio, then got a taxi back to where he caught the one coming out. He went into the hotel, where he saw his better follower was in the lobby. He went up the service stairs and directly down to the lobby from the floor above. The watcher looked relieved.

Clint told the woman at the desk to get him an airport taxi and checked out. He went back up to his room and got his bag. He was soon on his way to the airport. The stupid follower was right behind in another cab. He could assume the better one had the sense to stay a block or two back or that he heard Clint order the airport taxi and was there ahead of him.

He thought about the two followers. One so obvious it was almost comical. He laughed.

There was a big white 1978 Lincoln Continental

sitting in the parking lot across past the car rental agencies. He smirked. Follower two was standing in front of Hertz.

Clint had phenomenal peripheral vision. He never seemed to be looking at people he could watch closely.

He got out of the taxi and went in through the check-in door. Rodriguez was there. The follower came in less than a minute later. Clint looked at him and shook his head. Rodriguez asked what was the matter. He said that the guy was so damned amateurish it was truly unbelievable. He would probably be glad this boring job was about over.

"The other one was better, but not good. Did he ever find where I went when I gave him the slip at Romero's yesterday?"

Rodriguez was open-mouthed. "Er, where did you go? He didn't tell me you'd lost him."

"Her name's Elena. She lives on seventh close to Chavales. I'm not a celibate."

Rodriguez laughed. "I see it isn't exactly smart to use your misdirection ploy on you.

"Here's the package. I'll go back to the hotel. Call me when you're boarding the flight.

"There's one change. When you get to Miami the man that you called Gonzo at Mr. Santiago's house will meet you. He'll give you the ten thousand, then you will return here, immediately. The flight is booked and is one hour and ten minutes later. It won't be necessary for you to leave the airport.

"This is because of the incident before when the FBI man accosted you. We are being careful."

Clint nodded and went to his plane. He stepped back off when he saw the Continental leave the airport to use his cellular. He called Santiago. "Gonzo."

"What?"

"Gonzo is to meet me at the airport with the ten grand and I am to catch a flight out in an hour. Rodriguez knew about the phony FBI man."

"I see. You have kept your deal with me in a royal flush in spades. What time does your flight leave Tucumen?"

"They won't be there to see me. They think I'll go right through with it. One o'clock."

"I want to withdraw certain deposited funds. They're in an escrow account that is to be paid at one o'clock. As they don't know you won't be on the plane they'll go to claim it.

"You have the jewels?"

"Let's say I have a box. There are two ways this could be handled. One is that I would be robbed at the airport, second is that there aren't any jewels in the box. They would claim I substituted is why

I flew right back out."

"It will be that. If they set Gonzo up against me, they would never trust him to keep the deal with them. It will be handled. Who?"

"An ex-politician named Jimenez."

"You will handle that part? What about friends Rodriguez and Nando? Luis will take your instructions."

"Why, a certain fancy car that seemingly can't do any wrong will be stopped. There will be a short discussion with the passengers. Tell Luis not to be in that car. I doubt he would be. He doesn't know about it."

"I'll tell him to contact you immediately. You'll get your two million dollars. I understand that I may keep the items that were taken from you here?"

"That's the deal."

"I'll speak with you later, War. You have saved me a lot of money. I do appreciate it. I will not again attempt to remove treasures from Panamá."

Clint rang off and thought, then boarded. Tonio had this set up for Panamá City. It would be handled there.

His cell buzzed. It was Luis. "Santiago called. I am in Tucumen right now. They sent me to keep an eye on you and not be seen. I'll meet you when you land."

Clint agreed and shut off the phone for the flight – after a call to Tonio.

Clint got off the plane and saw Luis standing by the door to baggage. He waved and went to him.

"This is Sgt. Hernandez. He's to take you to the customs intense search room. Tonio has everything arranged and is waiting. He says the car in question will reach checkpoint in half an hour."

"It won't get there," Clint replied. "Let's see what this is about."

They went into the room. Clint took the box out of his bag. It looked like the first one. There were four huge jewels in silver settings inside. Clint scratched the side of a huge emerald. It scratched through the acrylic and into the stone.

"Paste?" Hernandez asked. "Isn't that what it's supposed to be?"

"No!" Luis cried, laughing.

"Yes!" Clint cried, also laughing.

"I don't...?"

"It's supposed to be paste for the setup. It's supposed to be real jewels for the delivery so far as the recipient is concerned."

"So they would claim you switched them. You weren't followed this time," Luis said.

"Uh-huh. Shall we get something to eat and call a mutual friend in Florida?"

"I don't see why not."

Clint sat back and grinned at Santiago. They were in the Hotel Europa in Panamá City.

"I was really fooled by them," Luis said. "I thought this was to be a sweet and easy deal. I never understood why they wanted to use someone else. We never needed to do that. It would work with any of us. It was to set you up to take the fall for a bunch of phony jewels."

"What happened to that person, the politician who was behind it?" Santiago asked. "I know Rodriguez and Nando were shot in some back alley or something."

"I had the Lincoln Continental followed," Tonio answered. "They turned off on a side-road before Tolé. The man in the police truck following them called and asked for instructions. I said to wait no more than five minutes, then to go in after them. They came back out in less than five minutes and went on. At Tolé checkpoint only Jimenez and the driver were in the car. My man was sent back to drive along that side-road. He found a wad of Indios looking at two bodies, two men who were shot execution-style in a ditch. We have police observation that they went into that road in that car and they never came out, though the car did. Very quickly.

Ex-Governor Jimenez is trying to make a deal. We get the treasure back and testimony as to which others were involved in its theft or he gets life. If we get it all, the mitigating circumstances will be that he killed two international criminals. He gets four years.

"He won't survive four years in prison. He is not liked by a number of prisoners who are there because he is a corrupt snake."

"And my good friend, War, is a famous private detective here," Santiago said. "Luis wishes to remain here. Tonio will arrange that he ganars permanent residency.

"It is a beautiful place. I walked on the street in David and had no least fears I would be, as Clint would likely say, 'knocked over.' People would actually stop to speak with me. They are honestly curious about me. I was honest with them. I told them I was a gangster in Florida and wanted to get away from it for awhile.

"They thought it was a joke, I suppose."

"No. They don't care so long as you leave them out of it," Tonio replied. "You would be happy here, I think. You could live a tranquil life. You are handsome and rich, so you could have a good wife or a thousand girlfriends. You would know all about the ten thousand scams people would try, people like you used to be. You could have fun turning the scams back on them."

"I think possibly so. I have spoken with a good Indio friend of Clint's in a place called Isla San Cristóbal. I am to purchase a place on the top of a mountain there where I can view the Caribbean Ocean and all the islands at breakfast. There is a man on that island I could swear I have met in the United States. He was a very powerful man, perhaps the most powerful, in the mafia."

"Manny?" Clint asked. "Several people have told me they think Manny's Marko Boccini. I know Marko and know he has an island in the Mediterranean and a place in Southern Spain.

"Manny does look like Marko would if he'd clean up some and learn how to talk where he doesn't sound like a cliche movie godfather."

"Yes. I spoke with Manny. He is a cultured person. He can talk very much like Marko, but uses terms that Marko never would. He says you have convinced people he was Marko twice in your cases. If he could say 'stuff' or 'junk' or 'crap' instead of 'materials' he could probably pull it off. Things like that."

(Manny Matthews was actually Marko Boccini. He had moved to the island to raise a family and escape from his life as a mafia don. He and Clint had been friends for some years.)

They chatted for awhile, then went around the city a bit. Santiago said he wouldn't care for the city anymore than he cared for Miami. He was going to try to spend at least six months of the year here.

Clint suddenly remembered something and said, "I'll be damned! I forgot!" He called Danny Betts and said he could go home.

In the morning Clint headed back to Quebrada Tula and his family two million dollars richer. The money would go, as had so much he'd gotten in his cases, to building schools and clinics for his people, the Ngobe.

And for an occasional helicopter ride across the country to be with his family!

C. D. Moulton's works are available on most major outlets as printed or e-books. CD writes the CD Grimes, PI, mysteries, the Det. Lt. Nick Storie mysteries, the Clint Faraday mysteries, the Flight of the Maita science fiction series, books on orchid culture and many others of many types. Mystery, adventure, intrigue, science fiction, humor, fantasy, paranormal, mild erotica, and factual.